Stamp Out

by

Ido Graf

I dedicate this novel to:

Mum

'Ultio est ferculum quod potissime apponatur frigidum.'
Revenge is a dish that especially ought to be served cold.
Latin Proverb

'Ultio est ferculum quod potissime apponatur frigidum.'
Revenge is a dish that especially ought to be served cold.
Latin Proverb

Also, by Ido Graf

In the Adam Wolf series:

'Eye Kill'
'Regina Blue' - Publication due in late 2023
'See Glass' - Repeated Amazon Best Seller in Multiple
Categories, internationally.

Short Stories:

'Ukraine Rising'
'Stamp Out'
'My Mercedes'
'Latin Jack' – Coming soon.

Media Requests & Film Rights

All press enquiries or film rights requests relating to Ido Graf's books should be directed to his publicist.

Any negotiations regarding the novels should be directed to his lawyers of choice in Washington D.C.

Please make any enquiries through the contact page.

https://www.idograf.com

ISBN: 978-1-9162140-9-5

Contents

Cast of Characters

Barristers
Giles Fitzmaurice KC - Head of Chambers,
    Lincoln's Inn
Philip Cavendish
Rupert Cecil
Charles Wentworth KC – Head of a rival set
Nirmal Kaur KC - Prosecutor

Clerks in Chambers of Giles Fitzmaurice KC
Senior Clerk Paul Bowers
1st Junior, Claude Philips
4th Junior, Tom Creegan

Recorder of London, Henry Farnsworth KC, Old Bailey

Marjorie, House Cleaner

Solicitors
Jack De Bailliencourt, Snipe, Bellows and Chomney.
  Senior Clerk's solicitor

**Police St Albans Central Investigation Department
  CID**
Detective Inspector (D.I.) Michael Cahill
Detective Constable (D.C.) Beddingham

Matron Phoebe Edwards

Media
Editor
Journalist of unnamed Newspaper based in Wapping

Prologue
14 Furze cul-de-sac, St Albans, Hertfordshire, U.K.

The evening drizzle had ceased. A cool breeze followed and wafted across the darkened suburban gardens wending its way over fences and through dense bushes and mature trees. The only sound came from the noise of the wind and the persistent rustling of the leaves punctuated by an occasional haunting screech from a ghostly tawny owl. As the light breeze cut through the night air it raced through the garden of the final house in the long cul-de-sac before making its way across open fields and on into the dense wood beyond.

Unseen, a human form, bottle in one hand and bag in the other, had crossed from the garden into the wood before disappearing among the trees and the foreboding shadows.

The property stood alone and in total darkness some

distance from its nearest neighbour. It was an impressive Edwardian structure which had been finished very much in the Art Nouveau style which had been popular in the Belle Époque. It was a substantial building with striking brick and stonework detailing. All seemed ominously quiet within the magnificent house, but all was not as it seemed.

In the more than one hundred years since the first stone was laid it had lost none of its elegance, though in the dark of a moonless night it seemed chilling. The garden was alive with leaves ripped from their branches and dancing in the breeze. Towards the rear of the extensive lawn stood an enormous sycamore which swayed rhythmically encouraged by the persistent gusts. Around its grasping roots great round holes burst forth from the badger sett below. It extended from the property deep into the field beyond and was said to predate the house by at least two hundred years. Only one badger ventured forth that night weaving its way backwards and forwards across the garden passing by the untidily open French doors with their billowing rain-soaked curtains. Beyond the void the room within lay ominous and unwelcoming. The available light, little as it was, gave up the shadowy outlines of a large television and antique furniture. All was as it should have been, all but for a leather recliner chair. It sat, partially extended, to the side of the room. In it lay a middle-aged man dressed in pyjamas and slippers looking as though he was asleep. In a deep sleep. A broken wineglass at his feet and an ugly red stain about it violating the opulent cream carpet.

Chapter One
14 Furze cul-de-sac, St Albans,
Hertfordshire, U.K.

The cleaner came, as she always did, promptly on the Thursday morning at 10:00 am. She picked up the post and went into the study, dropping the letters neatly onto the desktop as she did so. Feeling a little cold, Marjorie pulled her lilac lambswool cardigan a little tighter about her voluptuous, middle-aged body. She glanced around, enviously, as she always did, at the beautiful art, furniture and sculptures which adorned the majestic house. Then retracing her steps, she slipped into the kitchen where she made herself a coffee prior to starting work. Marjorie always enjoyed this part of the morning ritual as it made her feel as if she belonged there - the woman of the house. She ground the Jamaica Blue Mountain Beans by hand in the elegant Victorian grinder before brewing a cup of pure nectar. She could never afford coffee of that quality, so it was her treat to herself. The kitchen still oozed the exotic smell of the Blue Mountain as she put her cup into the dishwasher before setting off on her mornings work. Still feeling quite cold she looked about to see if her employer had left a window open. She doubted that he would have, as he rarely forgot anything.

Coming closer to the lounge Marjorie could feel a cold draft against her skin. The owner, before he left for chambers, had occasionally left windows open when he knew that she was about to arrive. He did this particularly when he had waited up late the night before smoking Cuban cigars, drinking French Claret, and listening to works by his favourite composer, Saint-Saëns.

Prior to taking up her post, she hadn't known anything about classical music, but she had made it her goal to learn once she had started working for him. Marjorie also learnt about the finest wines, foods, and cigars. All was done out of love. Not love for him – he was a brutish ogre. But more out of love for his money and his lifestyle. She was the best dressed cleaner for miles around and she always arrived lathered in Chanel perfume, which she could hardly afford. Marjorie had become adept at going to the posher areas of London and visiting the charity shops there. The cheap designer labels she had become so shrewd at finding added to her self-worth and she felt to her station. Often, she would buy blouses which were a size or two too small for her and which were also quite low cut. On the rare occasions when her employer was working from home she would wear them, taking every chance to show off her voluptuous body to him. She dreamed of marrying the bachelor and of instantly gaining a status which she could only ever aspire to. He on the other hand despised her for her low-class background, her cockney accent which she tried to cover up, and what he saw as her tarty style. He accepted that she was, however, a necessary evil as he did not wish to lay in squalor, and he would certainly never demean himself by doing the cleaning.

Marjorie 'definitely' was necessary that morning. As she walked towards the open doors, she glanced over at the leather chair and saw her employer stretched out in the part-reclined seat. The only indicators of a problem were the broken glass and the streak of wine across the floor – oh, and of course, the dagger that was buried up to the hilt in her employer's chest, surrounded as it was by other stab wounds!

The scream that she let out would have been the envy of many an Opera Diva. If her 'former' employer had been able to listen, then he may even have felt some sort of respect for her, but he could not, and he did not! She burst out of the open French doors and through the side-gate screaming as she did so, with blackened cheeks from the mascara which bled through the gushing tears.

Her horror was, of course, because he had clearly been brutally murdered, but also in large part due to her realisation that her years of grovelling and hard work had been for nought.

Chapter Two
Furze cul-de-sac, St Albans, Hertfordshire, U.K.

It was a neighbour who found the cleaner screaming incoherently in the cul-de-sac. Getting some sort of story from the woman's wild ramblings he decided to make the 999-emergency call to summon the police. Shortly afterwards officers were dispatched to the scene, as was an ambulance.

The police arrived promptly, as they felt affronted to find that such a killing had happened in an area of St Albans where, usually, the most heinous crime was only ever akin to littering.

Before she was given a sedative and taken to hospital, the officers got enough from Marjorie to understand that something was seriously wrong inside the house where she cleaned. As the woman was driven away the two constables entered the grounds of the property. They knocked at the front door and getting no response they skirted the building. Coming across the open French doors they entered carefully. Moments later they exited the room, reported the incident, and called for back-up. At the local police station, a call was made to Detective Inspector Cahill in the Criminal Investigation Department, commonly known as the C.I.D., 'Sir, there's been a murder in Furze Cul-de-sac. The Chief has asked that you attend the scene. There are officers on site.'

Cahill responded, 'Will do, Sergeant.'

The D.I. turned to Detective Constable Beddingham, who sat close by, and said, 'Come on let's go. We've bagged a murder!'

As Beddingham drove them to the crime scene, the D.I. knew that he was the obvious choice for this murder. Firstly, many of the other Detectives were away on courses or on holiday. Secondly, the few who remained had heavier caseloads than Cahill had. Finally, he was considered, by the senior officers, to be more refined and presentable than many of his other colleagues. And as this murder had occurred in one of the more affluent suburbs of town, his boss would want someone on the case who would 'fit in'.

Beddingham said, 'I'm surprised with the location. I doubt there has ever been a murder in that part of the city ...' then he laughed and said referring to its Latin past, '...not even in the Roman times!'

Cahill stared out of the window at the passing buildings replying, 'Well maybe it was about time! There are villains among the rich and not just the poor.'

Beddingham had always felt that Cahill was a cut above the rest of them and he wondered if the D.I. looked down on his colleagues. He was reassured to hear that Cahill seemed to be fair minded. By the time the detectives reached the property, three more police cars had already arrived with further officers. The detectives noticed that a forensic investigation team was also on site.

The DI spoke to the senior forensics officer and asked her to make sure she did a very detailed analysis as the victim was a high-profile barrister. He particularly asked her to dust for prints around the back door and the handles, inside and out. The forensics woman found his micromanagement mildly insulting, though she held her tongue.

Checking the property, nobody seemed to notice the missing bottle of a particularly fine claret, a Château Lafite Rothschild 1998, Premier Cru Classe. But then, why would they?

They did discover that the safe, which had a key lock, had been rifled and that some picture frames had been taken from the wall. It appeared that the frames would have held rare mail stamps as the few which had been left did so.

Over a kilo of cocaine was also found hidden under a cabinet in the main bedroom.

Near the French doors a picture frame had been dis-lodged from the top of a side-table and it lay on the floor with the glass smashed. The D.C. looked at it and said, 'Sir, it looks like whoever did this knocked the photo-graph while making their entrance or exit or in a struggle with the deceased. They probably trod on it in the melee. It looks like one of those end of year photos they take at those poncey schools.'

Beddingham looked around before continuing, 'Blimey this bloke must have had some real cash. I'd love to live here. No wonder someone targeted him!'

Cahill looked thoughtful as he said, 'Yes, he had a bet-ter life than the rest of us ...that's for sure. And whoever killed him really did a thorough job of it.'

Chapter Three
14 Furze cul-de-sac, St Albans, Hertfordshire, U.K

The officers knew that the pressure would be on. It was the murder of a high-profile barrister in a quiet cul-de-sac in a prestigious area - and the murder was particularly gruesome! The two detectives realised that the media would lap up the killing of a 'Fat Cat Toff!' They could sell copy for weeks or months on end. No doubt they would go into any salacious details they could dig up about the lawyer, his cleaner and anyone else in the firing line. The police would be a particular target. They always were. The force would probably be accused of ineptitude, incompetence, bias or anything else that the press could dream up.

The two detectives looked about the property and the actual murder scene. D.C. Beddingham had two of the constable's go door to door in the Cul-de-sac to see if anyone had seen something or someone unusual or if they knew anything of the deceased.

The senior forensics officer came to the D.I. after she had done her preliminary examination saying, 'It looks like the killer had keys or that he was welcomed in by the deceased.'

Cahill gave her a quizzical look, before responding, 'Why would you say that ...and if you were a betting person which option would 'you' guess was the one which occurred?'

'I just look for evidence, you make up the assumptions!' The woman replied with a slight laugh in her voice.

Then she continued, 'We can find absolutely no evidence of a forced entry. I suppose that the deceased could have left a door ...or the French doors unlocked, but I doubt it. If you look about the house everything is very exact. All is in its place. The cleaner had only just arrived, so I suspect the owner was a meticulous individual. It was quite cool last night and has been for the last week. All the other doors and windows are shut, which is as I would expect given the temperature and the fact that it was raining. Also, the fire still has embers. Why have the fire on and the French windows open – it doesn't make sense. He appears to have been stabbed multiple times by someone standing behind his chair. They then left the knife protruding from his chest. I think that the person entered with a key and that later they left the French windows open to cover up that fact. They may even have exited from the rear of the house.'

'Yes, I wondered about that!' the D.I, impressed with her summary, continued, 'Would you say it was a man?'

'Yes, I 'definitely' would. The power which was used to puncture the ribs and chest multiple times would suggest, as I am sure you would agree, someone very strong and 'very angry'.'

Detective Inspector Cahill looked thoughtful, saying, 'Yes, that is what I sense. So now we come to the 'who'?'

The forensics officer joked, 'Well that's your preserve ...thankfully! I will submit a formal report in the next few days once I have gone through everything.'

She began turning away when Cahill said, 'Did you find anything outside the house itself?'

She glanced back and said, 'The only thing of significance is a lone shoeprint. It was in one of the flowerbeds where it bordered the adjoining field. I believe it was left when the person vaulted the back fence when making their getaway. It is a good impression, as it was protected from most of the rain by an overhanging tree. We have photographed it and taken a cast.'

Then she continued on her way, satisfied with her work.

The two constables returned and the more senior one said, 'Sir, all the neighbours say that the deceased was very private and though he had lived here for approximately five years, they knew nothing of him. They said that there seemed to be no wife, girlfriend or kids and he very rarely had any visitors. None of them seemed to care for him and he was described as prickly, offish, and snotty by several of them. Even so, I wouldn't have thought that any of them would wish to kill him. They were all shocked and worried!'

The D.I. said, 'Thank you constables. Ok, well I think that we don't need you here anymore.'

'Right you are, Sir!' The senior constable said as they both left.

Cahill turned to Beddingham and said, 'Right, well if we accept that it was not a neighbour, partner or friend then maybe it has something to do with his work? Or maybe it has something to do with the drug trade? I have doubts that this is a straight burglary, given the brutality of the attack and the possibility that a key was used or that the assailant was allowed in by the deceased. I think that this crime may well be very personal in nature. I suspect that murder was the goal and theft was probably just an added benefit or was being used to give the impression of a burglary gone wrong. We shall see! ...Right then, you have a look around here and see if there is any information about his work, friends, or anything else and then meet me back at the station.'

'Fine, Sir!' Beddingham responded.

'Actually, I think I will go to the hospital first and speak to the cleaner, if she is coherent.'

The D.C. watched Cahill as he walked up the garden path before leaving and hitching a ride with a uniformed officer in one of the police cars.

Chapter Four
St Albans City Hospital, St Albans,
Hertfordshire, U.K.

The police car slid effortlessly into a parking bay near the Accident & Emergency entrance at the local hospital.

The D.I. stepped out and wandered nonchalantly through to reception. Flashing his identity card, he was passed on to one of the wards.

Arriving, he spoke to the Matron. Looking at her name tag on her uniform he noted that her surname was Edwards. She looked about thirty-five years old, was quite pretty and a little plump. She was very busy when he first spoke to her, but she made time for him. The Matron walked him to the private room where the cleaner lay in bed. A constable stood at the door of her room and as the D.I. and Matron entered, he nodded in recognition, saying, 'Sir!'

The Matron had a kindly disposition and she walked

over to the woman and gently cupped the cleaner's hand in hers, saying softly, 'I hope you are feeling better, my love. This Detective just needs a quick chat with you if that's ok? Don't worry, it will all be fine, and I will be nearby if you need me.'

The Matron turned to the Detective and gave him a wink as she left.

Detective Inspector Cahill also tried to put the woman at ease. Once she seemed calm, he began to question her. He took his time, and she did eventually give up some information. Most important was that the deceased had three sets of keys. He had one himself, the cleaner kept one and the final keys were at the deceased's chambers in his drawer. She explained that a single key opened all the doors in the house, and they were attached to a plastic fob with a Penny Black stamp design. The barristers set and the one he kept at chambers also had the key for the safe. The barrister had told her that if ever she lost her key, and he was away, then she was to contact the clerk at chambers, and he would get that set couriered over to her. She said that it had only ever happened once and that she had then found her keys, so she returned the other set to the clerk. The woman also recalled that she had never known him to be in a relationship and that he had few friends and kept away from his few distant relatives. Marjorie said that she had no idea who would want to kill him. The inspector felt that she had had quite a sweet spot for the deceased.

He wished her well and then, leaving, he had a quick chat with the constable who was on guard duty and then he turned towards the corridor. As he did so, he heard softly running feet and the musical sound of the Matron's voice calling out, 'Excuse me Detective. Um ...I just thought ...um ...that it might be useful if I had your number ...um ...just in case the patient remembers anything in future?'

Enchanted by her, he smiled back and said, 'Yes, thank you Matron. That would be helpful.'

He passed her his card and went to leave. As he did so, he half turned and said, 'Call any time ...day or night.'

'Yes ...yes certainly.' She replied in as professional a voice as she could as she beamed at him as he left.

Chapter Five
Chambers of Giles Fitzmaurice KC,
Lincoln's Inn, London, U.K.

The phone rang and a rough cockney voice called out 'Chambers of Giles Fitzmaurice KC. How can I help?'

The police officer said, 'I am Detective Constable Beddingham, from St Albans C.I.D. Can I speak to the Senior Clerk?'

'Yes, officer. I will transfer you now.'

The clerks' room was the beating heart of any barrister's chambers. The clerks managed the day to day running of the set and in particular the diary of cases which each barrister was to appear on.

Tom was the fourth junior and having put the policeman on hold he turned to Paul Bowers, the senior clerk saying, 'Paul I've got a copper on from St Albans C.I.D. He wants to speak to you.'

The Senior Clerk headed a team of juniors, with the

first junior being the most senior followed by the second junior and so on.

The set specialised in Defamation & Commercial law and therefore had nothing to do with the police. Paul looked thoughtful and said, 'Right put him through to me in Fitzy's room.'

He got up from his mahogany desk which he had been gifted by a retiring silk many years before and wandered through to Fitzmaurice's room which was next to the clerks' room. Fitzmaurice was at the High Court all day and wouldn't return until after 5:00pm. The phone started ringing as Paul entered the room and sitting down, he picked up the receiver, saying, 'Paul Bowers speaking. How can I assist you officer?'

The officer noted that though the senior clerk also had a cockney accent it had been softened by years of interaction with barristers and high-end solicitors.

'I am D.C. Beddingham from St. Albans C.I.D. I understand that Philip Cavendish of 14 Oak Crescent, St Albans was a tenant with your set. Is that correct?'

Paul noted the use of the past tense with some concern, 'Yes, he is a tenant in Chambers. Is everything ok?'

'I'm sorry to have to tell you, but he has been murdered.'

'What! ...murdered!'

'Yes, I'm afraid so. I would like to arrange a time when we can come over to your chambers with our forensics team. Please do not let anyone enter his room until we get there. Can we say 4:00pm this afternoon?'

'Paul was stunned. None of the clerks had ever liked Cavendish but murdered – that would be a shock to everyone!'

'Yes, certainly! We have two spaces in front of Chambers. I will reserve them for you.'

'Thank you. We will need to speak to you and possibly some of your colleagues about the deceased's movements in the last few days and to ascertain whether there was anything unusual going on in his life or if anyone might have wished to harm him?'

The use of the term deceased seemed quite cold as Paul replied, 'We will assist you as much as possible.'

They said their goodbyes and as Paul put the phone back on its cradle, he stared thoughtfully at it. Then he slipped quietly out of the room and upstairs to Cavendish's room.

Twenty minutes later he returned to the clerks' room holding a brief which he had taken from a shelf in one of the other barristers' rooms. He did not need the case papers, but he did not want the other clerks to think that he had been into Cavendish's room.

'What's going on Paul?' Claude, his first junior asked as the other juniors watched on.

Paul considered what to say before responding, 'Cavendish is dead.'

He breathed in deeply and continued, 'He's been murdered!'

The other clerks all stared at Paul in disbelief!

'Blimey what happened?' Claude questioned.

'I don't know! But the coppers are coming here today with a forensics team. Don't let anyone into his room until they have finished with it. I am going to send an email to everyone and then I will go over to court to see if I can have a chat with Fitzmaurice'.

Paul sent the email around then he took an envelope from his drawer and wrote an address on it before sticking some stamps on the front. He then left chambers, taking the envelope with him. Heading over to court, he slipped the contents of his jacket pocket into the envelope before dropping it into a post box as he passed by.

Chapter Six
Royal Courts of Justice, Strand, City of Westminster, London, U.K.

Fitzmaurice was furious. He didn't like Cavendish either. He also felt that his 'now' former colleague was completely untrustworthy.

The case was still going on, which was the reason that the Judge was beginning to nod off whilst listening to the tedious and copious case law which was being relied on by Fitzmaurice's opponent.

'This is damned inconvenient!' Fitzmaurice whispered over his shoulder as he chatted with Paul who was in the bench behind him.

'As you know I have applied to go on the bench, and I could do without this sort of scandal at this time. It's the sort of thing that could scupper my judicial application. Can't you get the police to come back on Saturday when there will be fewer people around?'

'I am not sure that would be advisable and anyway I think they would refuse, and it may even make them ...' Paul paused for a moment, for effect, before continuing, '...suspicious!'

Fitzmaurice regularly sailed to France and back in his magnificent, wooden Spirit Deckhouse Yacht. Whenever he returned, he did so with large quantities of Cognac, Armagnac, Champagne, and fine wines. Much of it was, later, laid down for investment purposes. Never paying the required customs duty, Fitzmaurice's stomach turned at the thought of the police beginning to pry into his leisure activities.

'Bloody hell! Yes, you are probably right. Well ...'

'Not disturbing you are we Cavendish?' the Judge, by then wide awake, enquired in a supercilious tone.

Fitzmaurice spun around, rose, and said, 'Oh, ...no My Lord! Please forgive me. Just had some urgent Chambers business to attend to.'

'Well, maybe you could wait until court rises before you discuss how many boxes of tea bags to order for chambers or whatever else you are discussing with your clerk?'

There was a general sniggering about the court including from Paul who had clerked the Judge many years before when he was at the bar.

'As you wish, My Lord.' Fitzmaurice begrudgingly replied.

Fitzmaurice sat down and the case resumed.

Paul waited a respectful few moments before standing and heading for the exit. Reaching the door, he turned and bowed and saw the Judge glance over at him giving the faintest of smiles to his former clerk, before Paul slipped past the oak door and disappeared.

Fitzmaurice spent the rest of his time in court in a cold sweat as he wondered where he could move the bottles which filled his cellar at home. 'Crikey, he thought to himself, I've even got some in bloody Chambers!'

He had a very vivid image in his mind of being dragged from his house by the police as he tried to scream his innocence.

Chapter Seven
Lincoln's Inn, London, U.K.

The forensics van arrived at the chambers just before 15:45 and the two-man team pulled into the parking space in front of the chambers. It had been a grinding journey through heavy traffic, and the driver was glad of the parking space, so close to the scene, as he had so much equipment to carry.

Five minutes later Detective Constable Beddingham pulled into the space beside them in an unmarked police car with D.I. Cahill half asleep in the passenger seat.

On the arrival of the detectives the forensics team alighted and began to get their kit ready. Cahill awoke and the two Detectives climbed out of the car, as the D.I. had a leisurely stretch to refresh himself. He noticed that many of the windows in the square around him were filled with barristers and their clerks looking on with interest at the forensics team, dressed in white overalls and what they all believed to be plain clothes officers who were with them. The Inns of Court were an intimate, Dickensian throwback where the majority of the barristers' chambers in the country were situated. There are four Inns, and they are called Inner Temple, Middle Temple, Gray's Inn, and Lincoln's Inn where the deceased had his chambers.

Cahill thought wistfully to himself, 'I wonder what my life would have been like if I had had the opportunity of becoming a barrister?'

Suddenly, a flight of pigeons noisily swooped down through the trees over the chambers before disappearing on towards Old Buildings. The swooshing sound of so many small wings beating in sync took him from his thoughts.

Beddingham, who stood waiting with the forensics lads, questioned, 'Shall we head on in then Sir?'

'Yes, let's get on with it.' The D.I. responded.

As they entered the ancient and elegant building two barristers passed them by on their way back to court. Their horsehair wigs, striped trousers and gowns which flowed behind them appeared quite normal in the surroundings.

Chapter Eight
Royal Courts of Justice, Strand,
City of Westminster, London, U.K.

Giles Fitzmaurice KC finished court, briefly spoke to his client and then privately with his instructing solicitor. Finishing up rapidly he left his large pile of law books in the robing room where one of the junior clerks, trolley in tow, would retrieve them before the building shut. Being a Kings Counsel or as they were commonly called by the clerks, a Silk, he wore a horsehair wig, a silk gown, court coat, waistcoat, and striped trousers. He looked imposing as he scurried out of the Royal Courts as fast as he could. He also looked very concerned.

It was a short walk through the passage beside Wildy & Sons, the historic Law booksellers. Coming to his chambers he saw the forensic van outside the chambers and muttered, 'Good heavens!'

Arriving at his Chambers he heard someone call over

to him in a sneering, cut glass accent. Turning he saw Charles Wentworth KC, Head of a rival set, 'Nothing wrong I hope, Giles?'

Fitzmaurice responded begrudgingly, 'I am not at liberty to discuss matters.'

As Giles disappeared into Chambers, Wentworth KC chortled to himself before carrying on to The Seven Stars pub on Carey Street where he was to meet a solicitor for a pint.

Chapter Nine
Furze cul-de-sac, St Albans, Hertfordshire, U.K.

The cul-de-sac was deadly quiet. The streetlights were sparse and gave some intermittent pools of light in the darkened street. In the shadow of a privet hedge a person stood, unmoving. They had been there for ten minutes, watching and waiting. Then the individual pulled back the sleeve of their rain jacket to look at the time. It was three in the morning. There wasn't anyone around and the only sound to be heard was the intermittent hoot of a tawny owl which perched, unseen, amongst the branches of a Scots pine.

Waiting a few more moments the watcher set off along Furze cul-de-sac. Wearing jeans, trainers, and the jacket with its hood up and pulled tightly over the face the identity was hidden. Keeping to the shadows where possible the person slipped into the front garden of number fourteen.

Then the person stepped close to a large beech hedge and waited and listened. Hearing nothing the intruder walked up the path to the front door. It had police tape across it to indicate that entry was forbidden. Taking out a key from their pocket the individual opened the door and ducked under the tape slipping into the house before silently shutting the door. The owl hooted once more as the intruder slipped into the study. Whoever it was, they knew their way around and what they were looking for. The police had thoroughly searched the building, but unknown to them there was a secret compartment hidden in the back of the bookcase in the hall. The intruder did, however, know of its existence. The person pulled the books away which obscured the compartment. Then the individual pressed the panel, and it popped open. Inside there was only one item. It was an ornate, leatherbound folder. The intruder slipped the item out and replaced everything on the bookshelf. Then they retraced their path heading back out of the cul-de-sac and then walked the fifteen minutes it took to get to their car which was parked several streets away.

As she got further away from the property a great smile spread across Marjorie's face.

Chapter Ten
Police Headquarters, St Albans, Hertfordshire, U.K.

Detective Inspector Cahill arrived back at the station and headed up to his office. The room was swelteringly hot, and he felt as though he was melting. The air conditioning had packed up two weeks before and they were still waiting for an engineer to come to fix it. He opened the window and the door to his room to create a welcome draft. Just as he sat down his phone rang.

'D.I. Cahill!' He answered in a musical tone which rose up towards the end.

'Detective Inspector it's Tomkins in forensics.' Came the response.

'Right, any news Tomkins?' He enquired.

'Yes, we've done all of our tests and the only fingerprints or DNA that we have picked up is for the deceased, the cleaner and our boys ...that is to say, with one exception.'

'What exception would that be?' Cahill responded.

'It's the door handles on the French doors, Sir. We picked up fingerprints on the brass on both the inside and on the outside.'

'Well then, we have our man ...er, or woman!'

'Yes, it looks like it, but though the prints are fresh and clear we have no record of them on the database. However, it is a man. I did a biochemical analysis and the amino acids in the sweat deposits which gave me this information.'

Cahill thought for a moment before saying, 'So the killer or should I say suspected killer has no criminal record. But, if it was someone from within his social circle or his workplace then we could expect that, couldn't we?'

'Yes, I would agree.'

'Also, we have manged to narrow down the footprint in the garden. It looks like it comes from an Adidas trainer.'

'Well, that narrows it down to probably several million people in the UK who own a pair. Hell! Even I have a set ...maybe it was me!' Cahill chortled to himself.

'Respectfully that is where you are wrong, Sir! This trainer has one side gouged out. Possibly a dog chewed it or maybe it got damaged somehow. Anyway, it makes it quite distinctive!'

'Well, that really is interesting.' Cahill said, before continuing, 'Fine, thank you Tomkins. If you get anything else, then let me know!'

Cahill put the phone down and looked pensive. She had done her work as he had expected - very well. A pencil lay on his desk untidily and he gently pushed it away with his forefinger as he thought about the sequence of events.

Chapter Eleven
Chambers of Giles Fitzmaurice KC,
Lincoln's Inn, London, U.K.

The detectives and the forensics team worked on the deceased's room. They did not find the keys to Cavendish's house that the cleaner had mentioned.

When Cahill questioned the Senior Clerk about the keys he responded, 'Yes, I knew that he kept spare house keys in Chambers and where they were. If they are not there, then I have no idea what happened to them.'

The officers noticed that the stamps in the frames on the barrister's walls were, in, colour photocopies, which did not seem in keeping with the man himself. The back of the pictures looked as though they had been tampered with some time recently. What Cahill and the other officers did not know at that time was that the originals which had hung on the wall were some of the most valuable which had belonged to Philip Cavendish. He enjoyed flaunting them before his lay and professional clients.

The D.I. had checked the pictures himself and he had the impression that the copies were relatively fresh. He was beginning to fit pieces together.

Cahill spoke to Fitzmaurice KC and asked, 'May we search the rest of the Chambers?'

The silk was outraged, 'Whatever for? You have no right to!'

'Sir, is there a problem? If you prefer, I can get a search warrant and come back again with more men on the next occasion?'

Fitzmaurice KC was pompous, and he had no wish to be the subject of further gossip about the Inns. However, his refusal my well make the detective suspicious of him or of a potential cover-up.

He said begrudgingly, 'Oh, very well! You know that you are wasting your time though!'

Cahill ignored his final quip saying, 'Thank you, most kind!'

The officers then proceeded to search the rest of the building. Cahill headed for the library and noted that there was a stand-alone copier in the room. It produced colour copies. He noted that it had run out of paper. Looking about he picked up a full ream and dropped it into the paper tray. On shutting it the copier sprung into life. He watched as a single sheet printed. It was a copy of one of the stamps in the picture frames. The D.I. looked about and seeing nobody else in the room he folded the sheet and put it in his pocket.

He next headed to Rupert Cecil's room which was next door. The D.C. had already started on it, and he was running through the bookshelf. Cahill walked over to the desk and began checking the drawers.

'What have we here!' The D.I. said in a congratulatory tone.

Beddingham turned around and walked over to the open drawer. Sat in the top were two keys on a ring. Attached to the ring was a plastic fob with a Penny Black stamp design, just like the one they had found at the deceased's house and the same as the one the cleaner had. Inside an envelope to the side Cahill also uncovered several rare British stamps.

'Well, well, well! He's been a very careless boy hasn't he!' The D.C. whispered.

'Get forensics in here.'

Beddingham slipped out of the door and reappeared a few moments later with the forensics team. The detective had already spoken to them, and they got down to checking the stamps, keys and the fob for prints.

'Take an impression of the keys and we can get a set made up, just to make sure they fit Cavendish's place. Then photograph what we have found. We will leave them in the drawer and see if he mentions them of his own accord. Can you put invisible marker on the keys and the stamps so that we can identify them if they are moved from here.'

One of the forensics boys said, 'Sure, I will mark the fob and keys. I will just mark the envelope the stamps are in rather than the stamps themselves, if that is ok, Sir? They look very valuable.'

Cahill replied, 'Right do that. Hopefully Rupert keeps them in the envelope.'

The two detectives then sat down with all the available clerks and barristers to informally discuss the death of their colleague and to see if any of them could shed any light on the matter.

Everyone was shocked and though there seemed to be little liking for the deceased, nobody could shed light on who might have killed him.

Cecil was not in and nor were several other tenants. Fitzmaurice did not want the police back and so it was agreed that he would arrange for the remaining tenants to go to the station to speak informally with the police.

Chapter Twelve
Police Headquarters, St Albans, Hertfordshire, U.K.

Rupert Cecil lived in St Albans and so it was hardly inconvenient for him to attend the police station. However, it did irritate him. He had known Philip Cavendish since they were at school and though they had always been close, he did not feel particularly distressed that he was dead.

He introduced himself to the Sergeant on the front desk in such a haughty manner that the officer could feel his fingers twitching as if they wanted to lunge for his truncheon. The Sergeant always used the term 'Sir' or 'Madam' when he dealt with people who entered the station, even if they were murderers or burglars. He always believed the maxim 'who was he to judge' what life they had had, and he felt that there was no need to make their situation worse than it was. However, he did not use 'Sir' with Cecil.

'Wait over there and I will call you when the Detectives are ready to see you.'

The barrister was infuriated by the policeman's tone, but he did as he was told and went into the corridor before sitting on a dirty, orange, plastic chair. The smell from the drunken and bloodied occupant of the chair next to him was pungent and overpowering.

Twenty minutes later the Sergeant called out, 'Rupert Cecil!'

Cecil, who was surrounded by several solicitors, drunken youths, and a man with a black eye, jumped up and went over to the front desk. The Sergeant glared at him and pointed off to the side saying, 'Interview room number 2.'

He objected to his name being called out in case any of the solicitors knew of him, but there was nothing he could say.

Cecil didn't like the Sergeants manner on the second occasion either, though he followed the direction and headed to the interview room. Going in he found it to be empty, so he walked over to the table and sat down on the chair in front of it. A few moments later Cahill and Beddingham entered the room. Cahill said affably, 'Thank you for coming in. We just have a few questions to see if we can get a better picture of the deceased and who may have wanted to kill him.'

Beddingham filled a glass with water from a carafe and carefully handed it to Rupert.

'It's a pleasure Detective Inspector.' Rupert replied suavely.

Beddingham explained his rights and that it was a voluntary interview. He also said that he could have a solicitor present if he wished, but Rupert declined.

The D.C. continued with the questioning. Cecil expected most of the questions and they caused him no discomfort until Beddingham asked, 'Can you tell us where you were on the evening when the deceased was killed?'

Cecil was flummoxed and he visibly reddened in the face. 'What on earth is going on here? Is this a formal interview? Do I need a solicitor?'

Both detectives looked overly surprised when he mentioned needing a solicitor. They said nothing for a moment before Cahill responded, 'We are just trying to eliminate people from our investigation. We are making no accusation. We do not feel that you need a solicitor ... do you?'

Cecil could have bitten his tongue. He picked up the glass and took a long cool sip. It probably was standard questioning and now he was giving them the impression that he had something to hide, 'Well, no ...no! I apologise. Cavendish was my friend since childhood, and this has all put me rather on edge.'

He waited for a moment while he composed himself before continuing, 'I divorced last year, and I now live alone. I believe that I worked on a brief during the evening had a glass of wine and then retired to bed at about 10:00. I can only give you my word for that!'

'That's fine, Sir. We understand.' Beddingham said dryly.

Rupert found his tone unhelpful, and he inwardly questioned what the detective meant by, 'We understand!'

Then Cahill continued, 'Do you know of anyone who may have wanted to kill the deceased?'

'No, certainly not ...well, that is to say ...there is one person who never seemed to like him ...but I am not sure that he would wish to kill him!'

The officers looked interested, and Cahill said, 'And who might that be, Sir?'

'The clerk. That is the Senior clerk at chambers. Paul Bowers. Cavendish had made it clear that he felt that he should be removed. Maybe it was him?'

Beddingham and Cahill passed a look between them which Cecil found hard to read, but some primeval sense within him made him feel nervous.

Cahill responded, 'Have you ever seen a key with a fob which has a Victorian postage stamp on it?'

'Yes, I believe Cavendish had one like that ...come to think of it I vaguely recollect that I saw the very same key in Bowers open drawer the other day when I was talking to him about my diary. I paid it no mind at the time but come to think of it I do find it a tad peculiar!'

Cahill and Beddingham turned to each other smiling contentedly before turning back to the barrister. Cahill said, 'Thank you for coming to see us. You have been most helpful.'

'I say, do you think it could have been Bowers?' Cecil enquired.

'We'll be in touch if we need any more from you, Sir.' Cahill said noncommittally.

Cecil left and the officers returned to their room. They walked over to the window and watched Cecil as he walked down the street happily swinging his umbrella as he went. 'Doesn't he look chuffed with himself sir!'

'Yes, he certainly does! Right get the forensics boys to check his glass in the interview room for fingerprints!'

'Get a search warrant for the chambers. We will play this man at his own game!'

Chapter Thirteen
Chambers of Giles Fitzmaurice KC, Lincoln's Inn, London, U.K.

The next day Cahill and Beddingham arrived at the Chambers unannounced. Fitzmaurice KC was working in his room on a tricky intellectual property advice. On being told of the arrival of the police he came out of his room and asked, 'What is the meaning of this!'

'Sir, I have a search warrant. We wish to search the clerks' room.'

'This is preposterous! I shall make a complaint about this to your superior!'

Fitzmaurice was not concerned about protecting the clerks. He sought only to protect his Chambers and his own reputation, which meant he had no other option but to stand up for the staff.

'Please feel free sir. However, I would be grateful if

you could ask your clerks to leave their desks and to stand by the wall.

Fitzmaurice KC was outraged. But he felt that discretion may be his best course of action, particularly as the boot of his car in front of Chambers was full of bottles of French wine from his room.

'Bowers can you move over here with your juniors, whilst this charade is conducted?'

Bowers and the juniors were stunned, but they all complied. The officers went straight to Bowers desk and within moments they found what they were looking for. The keys with the postage stamp fob.

Beddingham asked Bowers where they had come from and the clerk said, 'I have no idea!'

'Do you know what they are for?'

Deflated he said, 'Yes, they're the keys to Mr Cavendish's home.'

Fitzmaurice KC turned green and said, 'Now look here Bowers, I don't want you to say another thing until you have instructed a solicitor.'

Bowers did not get the opportunity to respond before Beddingham continued, 'Paul Bowers, I am arresting you on suspicion of the murder of Philip Cavendish. You do not have to say anything, but it may harm your defence if you do not mention, when questioned, something which you later rely on in court. Do you understand?'

Bowers was nonplussed, but he responded softly, 'Yes, I understand ...but I did not put those keys in the drawer.'

One of the uniformed officers handcuffed Bowers to the amazement of the juniors and the Head of Chambers. The officers then made a quick search of the rest of the building. Cahill and Beddingham checked Cecil's room and found that the keys and stamps which had been in his drawer previously were missing. Cahill said quietly, 'I want you to look into our friend Rupert Cecil's background and find out anything else that may be of interest?'

'Yes Sir!' replied Beddingham, 'Shall I do the same for the clerk?'

'Not for the present.' The D.I. responded.

The D.C. could not understand why they would not investigate Bowers also, though there was an impression that Bowers was being framed. However, he had worked with Cahill for years and he had come to understand that he was a very shrewd detective.

As the officers took Bowers out to the waiting police vehicle, Fitzmaurice KC stood at the door a look of disbelief on his face. He watched the two police cars drive away and thought that this incident would probably destroy his set and his reputation.

He was drawn from his thoughts by Charles Wentworth KC who had been watching the events from nearby with some pleasure. Wentworth called out, laughing as he did so, 'Cooey!'

Then mockingly he questioned, 'Is this some sort of reality show, Giles?'

Fitzmaurice KC turned towards him with a look of pure venom written across his face before he stormed off back into his chambers.

Chapter Fourteen
Police Headquarters, St Albans,
Hertfordshire, U.K.

Bowers had said nothing in the car, nor at the station. His leather belt was taken from him as were the shoelaces from his immaculately buffed Loake Oxfords. Next Paul's blue polka dot silk Charles Tyrwhitt tie was removed, leaving him looking quite comical in his blue chalk stripe suit and white shirt with its cutaway collar still buttoned to the top. He was led away to the cells where he waited for his lawyer to arrive. He knew that Fitzmaurice would sort that out, if only to save his own skin.

Though Bowers was very troubled by his predicament, he couldn't help but force a grim smile at the thought of how blue in the face Fitzmaurice must have been.

Sure enough, within the hour one of the partners of Snipe, Bellows and Chomney had arrived. Bowers knew of them. Everyone in clerking did. They were the top firm in white-collar crime. All their work was privately funded and came at a very high price.

Jack De Bailliencourt had a one-hour conference with Bowers. Finishing up, he said that he would see Bowers at 10:00 the next morning when the interview under caution was set.

But he would not see Bowers, neither the next morning, nor ever again.

An hour after De Bailliencourt had left the police station, the cell door opened. Cahill stood in the door looking at Bowers who lay on the bunk. The detective shut the door behind him, and Bowers sat up.

Cahill slipped his hand into the inside pocket of his jacket. The detective pulled out the folded slip of paper and passed it to Bowers. The clerk took the sheet and unfolded it. He stared at the A4 sheet unblinking. Looking up, eventually, at Cahill he heard the detective calmly say, 'I know!'

Bowers said nothing. He just looked aghast at the detective. 'Don't worry,' the detective continued, '...I am a friend! There were prints on the photocopies.'

Cahill watched Bowers, very closely. Then he said, 'Cecil has tried to frame you!'

Bowers suddenly looked utterly deflated, whispering through gritted teeth, 'I can't say I'm surprised.'

Cahill left Bowers to contemplate his predicament.

A few minutes later Cahill calmly said, 'I need your help ...and by helping me, you help yourself!'

Bowers looked down at the unfolded sheet of paper and then looked back at the detective who had stretched his arm out. Bowers gulped as he handed the photocopy of the postage stamp back to Cahill.

He remembered back to the day that he had taken the stamps in their frames from Cavendish's room once he had heard of his death. He had quickly photocopied them and then placed the copies back in the frames before re-hanging them. He knew of no close relatives who might claim the stamps and he felt that they would better serve to enhance his own retirement. He remembered posting them to his home just in case the police decided to search the place if, for some unknown reason, they spotted the theft. He knew at that point that he had sealed his fate and his heart missed a beat.

'The fingerprints on the photocopies had been wiped clean but the ones on the frames ...well, they were yours.' Cahill paused momentarily before continuing, 'However, I expect that you helped Cavendish to put them up on the wall ...didn't you?'

Cahill had placed excessive emphasis on the last two words.

'Yes ...yes, I did ...that's right ...I did!' The clerk stuttered in astonished reply.

He then looked on in stunned silence as Cahill tore

the sheet into pieces and put them into his pocket, smil‐
ing as he did so.

Bowers sighed deeply and said, 'How can I be of assis‐
tance Detective Inspector?'

Cahill stared into his eyes and calmly said, 'I'll be in
touch.'

Chapter Fifteen
Police Headquarters, St Albans,
Hertfordshire, U.K.

'Sir, I've got the results back on Rupert Cecil.' Bedding-ham said as he came into the office.

'Well, anything of interest?' Cahill enquired.

'Yes. He leads a very expensive lifestyle. After he divorced from his wife last year he became even more heavily in debt. He has two daughters, and they are boarding at Benenden Private School ...and cheap it ain't! Cecil is paying for all the school fees. He did not come out well from the settlement with his wife who turned vicious once she found that he had been cheating on her for years with her best friend.'

'Sounds like a really great guy!' Cahill mocked.

'Yeah, too right! I'm glad my sister never met him! He also has a new girlfriend, as the wife's friend dumped him to save her own marriage. His new woman is milking him dry so at least there is some justice in life! Expensive holidays, top restaurants, fine jewellery... the list goes on. His income seems to have dropped as his work has reduced. Also, he is behind on his HMRC VAT and tax payments. He certainly was an old friend of the deceased. They went to the same public school.'

'Same school, hey? That doesn't surprise me at all! OK, it sounds like there may have been a motive ... money. The death of his friend may also release up more work in chambers for him. In addition, if he got his hands on the deceased's stamp collection then he could quickly realise its value, tax free. Well done, Beddingham! What about his movements on the night of the murder?'

'I didn't pick his car up on any of the cameras, but he was close enough to walk. His phone didn't seem to move, and he made no calls, but then he would have been smart enough not to have taken the phone to the murder scene.'

'That's as I expected!' Cahill said cryptically.

Chapter Sixteen
Fleet Street, London, U.K.

Bowers was walking along Fleet Street on his way to work much as he had done for most of his career. Long gone were the national newspaper offices of his youth which had made the thoroughfare famous around the world. However, it was still a bustling and vibrant area. But on that day Bowers noticed nothing. He felt the weight of the world on his shoulders as he listened to the rhythmic slapping of the leather soles of his Loake's as they paced along the damp pavement. He was tough, but even so, he was rattled.

Suddenly a man stepped out of a doorway, blocking his way. The Clerk felt his body tense.

'Hello Bowers!' The man said in a casual tone.

The Clerk made no reply. But the man continued, 'Please follow me!'

Bowers reluctantly did as he was asked, and he followed the man into Hen and Chicken Court. It was the narrowest of alleys and it was a dead end.

The man was Cahill, and he walked ahead about five paces and then he turned and faced Bowers, square on.

'Cecil has done his best to frame you for murder!' Cahill said.

He waited a moment and let his words sink in.

Then he continued, 'I am your only friend in this! I promise you ...your 'only' friend!'

Bowers stared into the black eyes that glared at him ... and he believed.

'What should I do?'

'It is growing ever clearer that Cecil murdered Cavendish. He is a very shrewd customer. You need to play him at his own game, or you will be the one falsely convicted for this crime. You will be interviewed by my colleague, D.C. Beddingham. You will build a picture of growing envy and animosity between Cecil and Cavendish. Allude to Cecil's financial problems. Don't overdo it! Make no mention of this conversation to anyone! Oh, and send me half of the stamps – keep the rest for yourself. I doubt that we will speak again.'

'Right ...OK!' Bowers replied.

Cahill stared deep into Bowers eyes and then squeezing past Bowers as he walked away. As he did so he passed the clerk a small piece of paper.

Bowers called after the D.I. saying, 'Why are you helping me?'

Cahill glanced back responding as he continued on his way, 'We have to stamp out people like them.'

Bowers felt a cold bead of sweat slowly sliding down his spine. He also felt an immense sense of relief as he read the typed piece of paper he had been given. It said send the items here and it gave an address in St. Albans.

When he left the alley Cahill was nowhere to be seen.

Several days later he went to the police station in St. Albans having received a request from D.C. Beddingham. He attended the interview without a solicitor as he felt that he had better protection from Cahill than any lawyer could provide.

By the time the interview had finished, Bowers had left Cecil in a very difficult predicament. However, he left the Detective Constable very satisfied.

Chapter Seventeen
Hornet Way, Burnham-on-Crouch, Essex, U.K.

Paul had been released from custody without charge the evening before. In the morning he found the envelope which he had posted to himself the day he had heard about Cavendish's death. He pulled out the stamps which he had taken from Cavendish's picture frames in Chambers before he had replaced them with photocopies. As instructed by Cahill he kept half of them for himself and then posted the others to the address the D.I. had given to him in College Road, St Albans.

As he dropped the envelope into the post-box, he couldn't help but wonder what on earth was going on.

He also thought how very lucky he had been.

Chapter Eighteen
Park Street, St Albans, Hertfordshire, U.K.

Rupert had just made himself another cup of coffee and he was about to put a saucepan of porridge on the hob. He had woken an hour before and had lain in bed reading the Telegraph newspaper whilst drinking his first cuppa.

As he opened the kitchen cupboard to get a bowl there was a knock on the door. Irritated he wondered who could be calling so early. He turned the hob off and walked through to the hall before opening the front door. The grumpy look on his face suddenly turned to shock.

'What are you doing here?' He asked.

As he passed the barrister several sheets of paper Cahill said, 'I have here a warrant to search your property.'

'What! This is preposterous!'

As Cecil began to read the warrant Cahill and his men brushed past the barrister.

'Wait a moment! What is the meaning of this ...it is an outrage!'

'Please stay calm Sir!' Beddingham said compassionately.

'Calm! Bloody calm! I'll have the lot of you sacked for this!' Rupert bellowed.

Ten minutes later the D.I. called out, 'Sir. Please can you come in here?'

Rupert stormed into the study where Cahill had been searching.

As Beddingham and Cecil entered the room Cahill questioned, 'Can you tell me how you came by these stamps and where this cash came from?'

Rupert Cecil was stunned as he stared at the envelope full of old postage stamps and the large pile of used banknotes which lay beside them in a drawer in his desk. He said nothing for a moment and then snarled, 'I have never seen these items before. It is quite clear to me that you are trying to frame me!'

Beddingham rolled his eyes and Cahill laughed and gently mocked Rupert saying, 'Yes of course I am Sir! Now please tell me the truth?'

Rupert said determinedly, 'I have told you the bloody truth! I want to speak to my solicitor!'

Rupert's face had turned beetroot red, and he looked as if he was about to have a stroke. He glared at the officers in outrage, but also with a deep sense of foreboding.

Cahill then turned to one of the forensics team who had also entered the property and he said, 'Get those items dusted for prints please and check the envelope for the mark your team put on it?'

'Yes Sir!' the young woman replied.

Cahill nodded to Beddingham and the D.C. took out his handcuffs and read Cecil his rights. Rupert had turned a light shade of grey and for once remained silent.

Then Beddingham noticed a pair of trainers sticking out from behind a chair in the corner. They were very muddy and were the Adidas brand. 'Sir! Look over there!'

'What's that?' Cahill questioned.

Then he walked over to the chair and pulled it aside. As he did so, one of them rolled over, exposing the sole which had been damaged. Cahill turned to his colleague and said, 'Well done Beddingham!'

'So, what! They are mine! I wondered where they had gotten to!'

'I bet you did Sir!' Beddingham said sarcastically.

Poor Rupert would not get to finish that cup of coffee after all.

Chapter Nineteen
Chambers of Giles Fitzmaurice KC,
Lincoln's Inn, London, U.K.

The phone rang out and Tom Creegan answered it. He said, 'I'll put you through now.'

The fourth junior turned and looking at Paul he said, 'I've got Bob on from KBW. He said its urgent!'

Bob was the senior clerk at a prestigious criminal set in Kings Bench Walk which was situated in the Inner Temple. He was one of Paul's oldest friends and he had known him for over thirty-five years from when they had both been very junior clerks in an Admiralty set in Gray's Inn.

'Hi Bob!' Paul chirped.

'Hi Paul. Have you heard about Rupert Cecil ...he's been arrested for murder. The one that the coppers had arrested 'you' for the other day!'

Paul looked into the distance in a daze as his mind tried to process the new development. Then he said slowly, 'How do you know?'

'One of my tenants just called me from court. His instructing solicitor is with a firm who have just been instructed by Cecil. One of the partners is seeing him now at the police station.'

'Thanks for letting me know, Bob. Let's do lunch tomorrow at the Cheshire Cheese.'

'Sure, I'll see you there at 12:00.'

The Cheshire Cheese pub had stood on Fleet Street since the early fifteen hundreds and was a favourite haunt of Charles Dickens and Mark Twain among others and latterly of Paul and Bob.

Paul put the phone down and half laughed to himself. Turning to his juniors who were interested to know what was going on, Paul said, 'Cecil's in the nick! He's been arrested for Cavendish's murder!'

'Fantastic!' Tom blurted out as they all laughed. None of the clerks cared much for Rupert.

'I'm going in to see Fitzy! I'd better tell him the bad news!'

Paul's first junior Claude laughingly said, 'Good luck with that!'

Bob slipped into Fitzmaurice's room saying, 'Sir, I've got some more bad news I'm afraid.'

Fitzmaurice KC looked up from his brief and gave a

heartfelt sigh. 'How much worse can this week really get Paul!'

'One of my clerking mates has just told me that the police have arrested Cecil for Cavendish's murder. He's at the station now.'

'Good Heavens!' Fitzmaurice said as his face dropped upon the realisation that the week 'had' gotten much worse.

Paul looked at the silk and thought to himself that Fitzy had suddenly turned quite ashen faced. He had clerked Fitzmaurice for over twenty years, and he had grown very fond of him, despite his cantankerous and snooty manner.

Paul said, 'Are you alright Sir? Can I get you a cup of tea?'

'Am I all bloody right? A cup of bloody tea? Of course, I'm not alright! One tenant brutally murdered! My senior clerk arrested for that murder! Now a senior member of 'my' chambers arrested for that same murder. And him a public-school man! What has this world come to? My Chambers a laughingstock and my career is rapidly going down the proverbial lavatory! Of course, I'm not bloody alright!'

He paused momentarily staring half-crazed at Paul before continuing, 'To answer your question ...No Paul, you cannot get me a bloody cup of tea! I need something considerably stronger. Pass me the bottle!'

Paul looked over to where the head of chambers pointed. On top of a fine mahogany sideboard, he saw the bottle of Dalmore Sherry cask select 12-year-old single malt whisky. He knew that Fitzmaurice had been saving it for the, as he saw it, inevitable celebration when he was made up to the Bench. Paul grabbed it and picked up one of the Waterford crystal tumblers which stood nearby. He was about to turn back to Fitzmaurice when the silk called out, 'Take a glass for yourself too! I'm sure you need a drink Paul ...probably more than I do and that's saying something!'

Paul picked up the extra whisky tumbler and then placed the glasses and the bottle before Fitzmaurice before sitting in one of the two chairs which stood before the Head's vast mahogany desk.

The silk removed the cork and poured two large shots. Then thinking better of it he added another shot into each glass. The Kings Counsel silently passed Paul one of the tumblers. Then he picked the remaining glass up and fell back into his high-backed leather chair. Fitzmaurice looked longingly into the amber liquid which glinted in its cut-glass receptacle. Then he closed his eyes and brought the glass to his nose taking a long smell of the Highland single malt. He enjoyed the strong, sweet, nutty flavours. Then, to the surprise of Paul, he drank the whole glass in one gulp, poured himself another glass and then drank that more sedately. He next poured a third glass and sat forward as Paul sipped at his whisky. Then Fitzmaurice KC wistfully said as he sniffed his glass, 'Thank heavens for the Scots!'

The room was silent for a while as they both drank. Paul wanted to say something comforting, something inspiring but he could think of nothing.

Fitzmaurice held his glass out saying most pompously, 'Well, I suppose I should propose a toast!' He gave a gentle cough to clear his throat before saying, 'To Philip Cavendish. I wish I had never met him!'

He then clicked glasses with Paul and they both took a large gulp of the Highland malt.

Then Fitzmaurice looked at the floor and when he raised his gaze he said, 'I feel sorriest for you Paul. You deserved better than this. I'm sorry!'

Paul's heart sank as he saw a great man destroyed before his eyes and yet his final concerns were not for himself, but for his clerk.

Paul looked at the broken man and, in that instant, he realised what he had always known. That the man he had clerked all those years was truly great!

Three hours later the junior clerks telephoned for a couple of London black cabs, and they then poured the head of chambers and the senior clerk into their respective vehicles before sending them on their way home.

As Fitzmaurice KC was helped into the cab, he could be heard by all in Lincoln's Inn as he bellowed out a bawdy sea shanty which he had learnt whilst studying law at Oxford.

Looking out of the window of the clerk's room in his own Chambers, Charles Wentworth KC sneered at the appalling scene saying, 'I always knew that Fitzmaurice was an absolute scoundrel!'

Wentworth happily slithered back to his room. Then he placed an anonymous telephone call to one of the seedier tabloids.

The tip-off was most welcome!

Chapter Twenty
Wapping, London, U.K.

The young man burst through the door of the glass walled office. 'I've got a real beauty, Sir!'

'Well, what is it?' The harassed editor lazily snarled.

'You won't believe it!' The young journalist said effusively.

The editor sat back in his chair, slowly rolled his Cuban Montecristo N°4 in his fingers before taking a leisurely puff on his cigar, savouring the moment and the smell of the tobacco. He had been in the game for forty years and editor for nearly twelve. He had seen it before all and yet he still hoped that he could be surprised. 'Well go on then!' he cried out.

'I've had an anonymous tip about the murder of a barrister called Philip Cavendish who was at a set in Lincoln's Inn.'

Interested, the editor snapped, 'What set?'

The young journalist was slightly taken aback, 'Well ...it's the Chambers of Giles Fitzmaurice KC.'

A wide smile slowly spread across the editor's face as he enquiringly said, 'Tell me all?'

'Well, I got a call a few hours ago from a very posh sounding bloke. He wouldn't give me his name, but I bet that he was a barrister or a solicitor. He told me a story which I didn't, at first believe ...until I checked into it. I now think that it is true. Anyway, it appears that this other bloke Cavendish was brutally murdered in his home in St Albans last week. The police initially arrested his clerk for the murder. Then they released the clerk and now they have arrested a friend of the dead barrister called Philip Cecil. He's a tenant in the same set.'

'This just gets better and better! Go on!' The editor chortled.

'Well, apparently, after this occurred, the clerk and the head of Chambers Fitzmaurice KC were seen being carried out of chambers by the junior clerks and thrown into a couple of taxis. The caller said that they were completely, in his words, 'blotto'. I've yet to verify this, but the caller went on to say that Giles Fitzmaurice KC turned the air blue when he was stuffed into his cab as he was singing filthy sea shanties. The sound echoed all around Lincoln's Inn according to the snitch.'

The editor sat back in his chair and rolled the cigar in his fingers once more. He was chuckling to himself and muttering something under his breath. Next, he took a long, slow puff on the Montecristo whilst savouring the exotic flavours. Then he blew out three smoke rings in quick succession while looking up at the ceiling.

The young journalist wondered if the editor was back on cocaine. There were many rumours floating around the office about the boss's past excesses and he certainly seemed to be acting peculiarly.

There was an embarrassing silence before the editor said, 'You were right ...I wouldn't believe it! But I really do want to believe! That stuck up git Giles Fitzmaurice KC and his tenants have had their claws into me on several occasions over the years with their bloody libel claims. Now it's payback time. Reallocate all your other work. I want you to concentrate on this story. And remember the more salacious or outrageous the story the better. Just make sure that it is true!'

'Yes, Sir!' The junior journalist excitedly said before he swiftly turned to leave.

'By the way ...' the editor continued as the man looked back, '...very well done!'

The next morning the story broke and the headlines ran, 'DRUNKEN TOFF SINGS LEWD SONGS AS BARRISTER PAL IS BRUTALLY SLAUGHTERED!'

As Charles Wentworth KC walked past the news-stand at Kings Cross train station the next morning on his way to Chambers, he noticed a large crowd buying up the morning editions. He joined the throng and bought his own copy. On reaching his chambers he grabbed his new briefs from his pigeonhole in the clerk's room and then rushed to his room to read the gory details. He was ecstatic with joy! The article was scandalous, though it cleverly danced its way along the safe side of the libel laws. Wentworth thought to himself that any reader would conclude that the set was populated with public school oiks who were getting what they deserved.

It was early but Wentworth pulled a bottle of Harvey's Pedro Ximénez thirty-year-old Sherry from the walnut cabinet to his side. The silk poured a liberal glass and then toasted himself before gradually savouring its flavours.

'It's going to be a great day!' He contentedly thought to himself.

Chapter Twenty-One
Police Headquarters, St Albans,
Hertfordshire, U.K.

Rupert's solicitor had been given 'pre-interview disclosure', which explained the reasons for Cecil's arrest and details of the offences.

She advised Rupert on the law, his possible defences, and the strength of the evidence against him. The solicitor asked for Rupert's version of events and then explained the options available to him during the interview. The barrister was very difficult to deal with and was extremely hostile. The solicitor tried to calm him down and suggested, given his conduct, that it might be more appropriate to give the police a prepared written statement and then to answer 'No comment' to all of the questions.

Given the evidence and his demeanour the solicitor didn't fancy his chances at the hands of a jury.

They agreed the statement which the solicitor toned

down. It purely denied culpability and also denied any knowledge of how Ruperts prints had gotten on to the doorhandle. As to the appearance of the keys which had been in his drawer and miraculously appeared in his clerk's drawer, he was evasive. It also denied knowledge of the trainers, the stamps and the cash which had been found at his home.

'Sir, I've checked the stamps and the cash we found at Cecil's house.'

'And?' questioned Cahill knowingly.

'We found no prints or DNA of use.'

'That's as I expected. Our friend Rupert is a very shrewd individual. And the envelope?

'Yes, the mark we put on it in Chambers was there.'

'And the trainers?'

'Well, it's not like a fingerprint but I would say that it is the same trainer that made the print in the flowerbed. The damaged sole is an exact match, but the soil on the trainers also exactly matches the soil in the flowerbed.'

'Right, thanks!' The D.I. said as the forensics woman disappeared off.

Cahill jumped out of his chair and headed down to the interview room where Beddingham was about to start the interview with Cecil.

The D.C. had just made himself a coffee before he bumped into Cahill in the corridor. 'Can I get you a cuppa, Boss?'

'No thanks. Let's just get on with it.'

'Right you are!' Beddingham retorted.

They went into the interview room and Cahill sat down. Rupert and his solicitor were already sitting on the other side of the table.

'Can I get you a drink?' Beddingham asked.

Rupert ignored the question but gave Beddingham a withering look.

'No thank you.' His solicitor replied.

'I am D.C. Beddingham and this is D.I. Cahill...'

'I already bloody know that!' Cecil butted in.

Everyone ignored his petulant outburst.

'I understand that you have been informed of your rights by the custody officer?' Beddingham continued civilly.

Rupert ignored the question, but his solicitor filled the embarrassing silence with, 'Yes, that is correct.'

'You have been arrested in connection with the murder of Philip Cavendish and for theft of valuable stamps which belonged to him.'

Rupert snorted in a demeaning manner and said, 'This is quite clearly a fit up by you two!'

The solicitor winced and Beddingham ignored him before continuing, 'You are speaking to us voluntarily and as such, if you wish to remain silent or answer 'no comment', you may do so.'

The D.C. continued, 'Whatever you do say will be

recorded and you should know that that recording is likely to be used in court as evidence if you plead not guilty to the offence.'

As Beddingham said this he turned on the recording machine.

Next the D.C. gave Rupert the caution, saying, 'You do not have to say anything. But it may harm your defence if you do not mention when questioned something which you later rely on in court. Anything you do say may be given in evidence.'

The solicitor interjected, 'My client has prepared a written statement and he will go 'no comment'!'

As she said this, she handed the statement to the D.C. who quickly read it. He then passed it on to Cahill and as he did, he displayed the faintest change in his expression which indicated to the D.I. that he didn't believe what he had read.

Cahill gave the statement a cursory glance and then said, 'Right let's get started!'

Beddingham then began asking questions to further their investigation, but as previously notified, he only received 'No comment' from Rupert.

They concluded the interview and Rupert had a short conference with his solicitor to discuss his situation. During the meeting, matters became quite tense as the solicitor tried to impress on him the grave difficulty that he was in. The solicitor also found it implausible that the police were framing him for the murder and said that a jury was likely to decide the same. At that point Rupert flew into a tirade and sacked the solicitor. As she left the police station she did so with a happy heart. She believed that he was guilty and that acting for him would be a complete nightmare.

An officer then took Cecil back to his cell.

The detectives then discussed the interview. 'That man is obnoxious! He's clearly lying!' barked Beddingham.

'Quite! He is definitely a liar!' replied Cahill.

He thought for a moment and then said, 'I'll get on to the CPS. We need to get moving on this.'

The Crown Prosecution Service agreed that there was enough evidence for a conviction and Rupert was formally charged with murder and theft. He was remanded in custody to appear at court the next day as the lengthy process began to bring him to trial.

Chapter Twenty-Two
A rented one-bedroom maisonette, Gorham Drive, St Albans, U.K.

Marjorie read the article in the newspaper which reported on the death of her employer. She had always dreamed of marrying him and of getting her hands on his lifestyle and more importantly his money. That would never be. Or would it?

She walked over to the table and sitting down she began to flick through the ornate, leatherbound folder which she had retrieved from her late employer's house, so early in the morning, many weeks before. She had been cleaning the house one day when she passed the door of the study and, unnoticed by Cavendish, she had seen him hiding the folder. Marjorie knew what was in it as she would often see him gloating over the contents. It was full of rare British stamps. She had become an expert on stamps through study whilst at home. Marjorie knew that the stamps were worth a great deal of money. She also knew that she would be able to easily realise the value by breaking the collection up and selling them off to dealers – cash of course.

The previous weeks had been spent calculating their value. It came to approximately two million in sterling. Marjorie was overjoyed. She would wait a year before she started selling the stamps, and then she planned to dispose of them ...slowly.

Marjorie picked up the cup of tea she had just brewed and smiled to herself. She would have the life which she had always dreamed of and best of all she thought, '... without being married to that unbearable snob, Philip Cavendish.'

Then she began to copy his handwriting from the Counsel's notebooks and other documents she had taken from his house over the years.

Chapter Twenty-Three
Old Bailey, Central London, U.K.

Cecil was committed from the lower Magistrates court in St Albans for trial at the Crown Court. His attempts to prevent his committal had failed miserably. Ordinarily he would have been tried at St Albans Crown Court but those in authority deemed his case so scandalous that it was sent to the Central Criminal Court of England and Wales, commonly referred to as the Old Bailey. It was located in central London. The hearing was to be tried by the Recorder of London, Henry Farnsworth KC, who was the most senior permanent judge of the Central Criminal Court.

The media were in a frenzy over the case. Several of them had suffered at the hands of barristers and in particular the tenants in the chambers of Giles Fitzmaurice KC. They roundly felt that it was time to get their 'pound of flesh!'

And they had so much to work with.

There was the murder of a top barrister in a sleepy suburb of affluent St Albans. What appeared to be the attempted framing of a loyal and working-class barristers' clerk. The arrest of a barrister, in the same chambers as the deceased, for the murder. Many of the players came from top British public schools – toffs as the press loved to call them. And then there was the theft of what was said to be millions in rare British stamps. The drunken conduct of the head of chambers and his singing of lurid songs had gone viral. It had morphed on social media into a band of villains and cutthroats who held booze and drug fuelled orgies in chambers while swilling vintage ports and wines. Even the cleaner had become a minor celebrity! She began to enjoy the attention of journalists and by the time she had finished giving her version of events she had really done a number on the three barristers who came in for the most abuse. She gave the impression that the deceased, Philip Cavendish, had been besotted with her and that he had repeatedly begged her to marry him. Marjorie suggested that she had refused because he was ashamed of her lowly status, and because he wanted the proposed marriage kept a permanent secret from his posh friends. She even claimed that he had repeatedly said that he wanted to leave all his possessions to her if he were to die. Marjorie implied of Cecil that he was jealous of Cavendish and that poor Rupert wanted her for himself. There was the suggestion that she was one of the 'other women' who were the reason behind Rupert's divorce. She even went so far as to imply that the murder may have been a 'crime passionnel' as the French so eloquently call it - a crime of passion. She went on to implicate Giles Fitz-maurice KC who she alleged also lusted after her. Though the members of the media found these lurid suggestions hard to believe it did not stop them from re-porting her words.

Even before the trial started the press headlines were asking of the defendant, 'Is this the vilest man in Britain?'

Rupert was driven from Wormwood Scrubs Prison, where he was held on remand, to the Old Bailey. He had been unprepared for the ferocity of the abusive heckling and screaming which greeted the van as it pulled into the court. The press had whipped the populace up into a frenzy for day one of court.

This entrance had unnerved him but not as much as when he entered Court No 1. He had rarely been inside a criminal court. Most of his work was on paper with the occasional case going before the more sedate civil courts.

Court No 1 was absolutely packed. The public gallery was filled with what could easily be described as a baying mob. Even the police, prison officers, court clerks and the ushers seemed to sneer at him. He felt that this was a very unhealthy start to the process. He wanted to scream out the age-old maxim, 'Innocent until proven guilty!'

But even he knew that it had been replaced by the modern-day trial by social media maxim, 'Guilty and never proven innocent.'

Confident to the point of arrogance, as a norm, he suddenly felt intensely unnerved.

Cecil had decided to defend himself without the aid of a solicitor or a specialist criminal barrister. Though nobody wished to act for him, even so his snub had greatly infuriated members of the criminal bar and the judges. Never a trusting man, Rupert had lost all faith in the Bar and lawyers in general who he felt had, *en masse,* turned against him.

Cecil sat waiting for court to commence. He was being prosecuted by an all-woman team. Nirmal Kaur KC was the leader, and her junior was Phoebe Briers who was in the same chambers as her. Behind them sat various members of the CPS and they in turn were surrounded by piles of lever arch files and law books.

The court clerk called out, 'All rise!' as the Judge came in.

Everyone stood and bowed. The judge gave Rupert a withering look as he thought of the age-old adage, 'He who represents himself, has a fool for a client.'

As the judge sat, and under his breath, he muttered to himself, 'How apt!'

The jury had not yet been called into court. The Judge heard preliminary legal arguments from the Crown Prosecutor and from Rupert. Rupert made an application to exclude some of the Crown Prosecutor's evidence and witnesses, but the Judge was having none of it. During these preliminary arguments, Cecil formed the view that the Judge was very hostile towards him, and he began to feel a sense of impending doom.

Neither Nirmal Kaur KC, for the prosecution, nor Rupert chose to challenge any of the jurors. Therefore, the twelve jurors having been agreed upon, each one was then sworn in by oath or affirmation, promising to, 'Faithfully try the defendant and give a true verdict according to the evidence.'

The judge then instructed the jury, advising them that they were expected to decide the case based upon the evidence presented to them in the court proceedings. He explained that they could discuss the case among themselves, but that they could not discuss it with anyone else who was not on the jury.

The jurors had already been warned that they could be found in contempt of court if they acted improperly. This could include using social media, the internet, or if they spoke to anyone outside the court process to obtain information about the case or if they tried to contact witnesses.

Nirmal Kaur KC gave her opening speech. The prosecution silk explained what the case was about, including the charges which Cecil faced and the case that the Crown had against him. At that point the jury were handed copies of a document, the indictment. This set out the counts or charges. During the opening the Judge repeatedly gave Rupert contemptuous glances as did everyone in the court.

Rupert inwardly cringed as he looked at the jury. He could not see a friendly face among them as they heard the damning case against him. He had to begrudgingly accept that Nirmal Kaur KC was immensely talented, and her delivery was silky smooth. The footprint, the stamps, the cash, the testimonies ...the list went on. His stomach turned as he thought to himself, 'How on earth have I gotten into this situation, even I would convict on this set of facts!'

The Judge was effusive as he commended Nirmal Kaur KC on her fair and balanced opening. Following the prosecution's opening, Rupert was given the opportunity to address the jury to set out the statement of issues in the case. At that moment he put forth his points of dispute in relation to the prosecution case. He re-iterated his assertion that the clerk, Bowers, possessed the keys to the house where the defendant had lived and suggested him as a possible culprit. He claimed that the mark on the keys and the envelope had been added after the keys had been found in Bowers possession and after the search of his home. Rupert's continuing attack on the police and the suggestion that he was being framed went down very badly with the judge. Judge Farnsworth KC warned him about making allegations which may later be found to be false. He told the defendant that he would take them into account during sentencing if he was found guilty. The judge also spoke to the jury and said that the allegations were being made about two serving detectives who had exemplary records and as far as he could see, no reason whatsoever to act in the way Cecil alleged.

Next the judge informed the jury in relation to the relevant law and any legal issues which they might expect to encounter.

As the Prosecutor began to present her case to the court matters went from bad to worse. Nirmal Kaur KC called her first witness. The senior clerk. Bowers was duly sworn in. She examined him directly while he was under oath. In describing Cecil while giving evidence, Bowers, unhelpfully Cecil thought, gave a portrait of a man who was a sexual predator who was excessively jealous and who had an explosive temper. Bowers also implied that he had always found him untrustworthy, and he knew that Rupert was riven by debt, particularly since the break-up of his marriage. Bowers said that Rupert was immensely envious of Cavendish's wealth, and he implied that Rupert had an intense interest in the value of Cavendish's stamps.

Rupert visibly seethed as he listened to his former clerk's evidence. Unfortunately, the look on Cecil's face only served to confirm the view the jury and the judge already had of the defendant.

Rupert's cross-examination of Bowers did not improve matters as he could hardly control his anger while he asked the witness questions. Bowers dislike of Cecil was palpable and gave a gritty honesty to his testimony.

Bowers was followed by Marjorie, the cleaner. She was giving evidence from behind a privacy screen as she 'claimed' that she was fearful of the defendant. Nirmal Kaur KC elegantly worked the witness. Marjorie was portrayed as timid, fearful, devastated, and emotional. She even had members of the jury in tears with her performance. Before Cecil cross-examined Marjorie he was warned to be sensitive by the judge given the witnesses fragile state. Rupert was unable to comply. His outrage and his anger could not be reined in. The judge repeatedly interrupted him which only served to make matters worse. It also gave Marjorie time to concoct her answers.

If there had been any chance for poor Rupert, then his shambolic and vengeful cross-examination of the detectives and the forensics officer finished him off. Some members of the jury were openly laughing when he suggested that he was the victim of an elaborate conspiracy between the police, the cleaner and the clerk. Others still rolled their eyes or stared at him in disgust.

As the judge watched their reactions, he couldn't help inwardly grinning like a Cheshire cat.

Once cross-examination of the final prosecution witness had been completed by Rupert, the Crown chose not to redirect their examination of the witness to cover any issues arising from the Cecil's line of questioning. Kaur KC felt that Rupert had aided her quite well enough already. All the prosecution evidence having been presented, Nirmal Kaur KC then stood up and plainly stated, 'That is the case for the Crown, My Lord.' Then she sat down, satisfied with the case thus far.

The prosecution case completed, and their evidence presented, Rupert was able to respond to the Crown's case and to give evidence himself. Cecil was in a terrible predicament, but even so he gave a good account of himself. However, it was one that nobody was prepared to believe. Nirmal Kaur KC cross-examined him with great skill. Teasing out inaccuracies and painting him as an inveterate liar who had tried to frame his own clerk for a murder which he himself had committed.

Punch-drunk after the onslaught from the prosecutor, Rupert stood unsteadily as he said, 'That is the case for the defence, My Lord'.

As he spoke Rupert noticed the sneer written large across the judge's face. Exhausted by the strain of the case and his own pessimism he fell back into the bench.

It was 16:20 and the judge said, 'I think that this is an

appropriate time to adjourn. Court will re-commence at 10:30 tomorrow morning for closing speeches.'

Then the court clerk spoke out, 'All rise!'

Everyone stood and bowed as the judge left the court.

Rupert was driven back to prison where he spent a very uncomfortable night. He hardly slept as he tried to formulate his closing in his mind. At 04:00 he rose from his bed and began to draft his closing. He found it immensely difficult to write as he felt that it would ultimately prove futile. Cecil may well have been an unpleasant character, but he was also a realist. He knew that, failing a miracle, he was doomed.

As he ate breakfast before being taken to court, he couldn't help but feel that it was the last meal of the condemned man. Looking into the bowl of lumpy porridge he doubted that it would have been his preferred choice if facing the hangman's noose. Then his heart sank as he thought to himself that he would need to get used to eating it.

As the van arrived at the court Rupert was met, once more, with banging on the exterior of the van and abusive chanting.

The guard who sat with him said sarcastically, 'Blimey, you're popular mate!'

Rupert ignored him.

Sitting in court awaiting the arrival of the judge, Rupert was acutely aware of the eyes of everyone in the room trained on him. There was also a constant hum, as people muttered to each other.

Nirmal Kaur KC entered the court with her junior and her CPS entourage. She nodded at Rupert, saying, 'Good morning, Cecil.'

Rupert looked up at her and replied sadly, 'Is it?'

She said nothing in reply and sitting down, Kaur KC turned to her team and became engrossed in animated, hushed conversation with the more senior CPS representative.

The court clerk called out, 'All rise!' as the Judge entered.

Everyone in the court rose and bowed to the judge before he sat down.

Nirmal Kaur KC gave her closing speech on behalf of the Crown summarising the facts of the case. She explained in detail why the defendant should be found guilty on the indictment and then she asked that the defendant be given life with a substantial minimum term.

Cecil felt utterly deflated by the time she had finished. He knew by that point that it had been a serious mistake to run his own defence.

However, he rose to address the jury and to conclude his case. Rupert set out the reasons why he should not be found guilty and then he tried to point out weaknesses in the Crown's case. Though he had little to work with, Cecil gave it his best. The case against him was strong and he had to accept that his allegation that he was being framed, whilst honestly believed by him, was probably implausible to the jury. He looked back at the members of the jury as he spoke and could see disinterest, loathing and distrust written across their faces.

Court then rose and re-commenced after lunch at 14:00.

Judge Henry Farnsworth KC looked at the public gallery and noticed a man who was tucked in the back row and who was trying to shield his face with his hand. Sneering, he said coldly, 'Good afternoon, Giles. Here to provide moral support for a colleague, are we?'

Giles Fitzmaurice KC's cheeks went beetroot red and half rising he mumbled something incomprehensible and then sat back down as the judge chuckled to himself.

Following the judge's comment, Fitzmaurice found himself to be of unhealthy interest to the members of the great unwashed who sat with him in the public gallery.

The judge instructed the jury on the law and then he went through the elements of the case. He explained that the Crown had to prove each of the elements for the defendant to be found guilty. He then gave the jury specific directions that they had to follow to come to a verdict. After Farnsworth KC had instructed the jury, he summarised the case for them so that it was fresh in their minds when they retired to deliberate. Then the judge asked the jury to appoint a foreperson and he told them that they must come to a unanimous decision on each of the counts of the indictment.

The jury retired and the matter was adjourned whilst the court awaited their verdict. Court commenced again fifty minutes later as they had indicated that they had come to a unanimous decision.

When the foreman rose to give the verdict of the jury the silence in the courtroom was intense. Cecil's heart was pounding like a drum as he stared agasp at the standing juror. Then the man spoke, 'We find the defendant guilty on all counts.'

The public gallery went wild. People cheered and hurled abuse at Rupert who sat mesmerised by what he had heard. The judge took five minutes to bring them under control and three onlookers had to be ejected from the courtroom in the process.

Rupert stared up at the judge who appeared to be gloating like a vulture sitting over a freshly killed carcass.

Then Judge Henry Farnsworth KC proceeded straight to sentencing. The judge spoke of the defendant's previous good character and of aggravating features such as breach of trust, the violence of the attack, his attempt to implicate his own clerk and the police. Following the sentencing guidelines, he gave Cecil a life sentence with a minimum term of twenty-five years.

As the Judge made his way down the corridor behind the court on his way back to his room, he passed the listing officer on her way to one of the other Judges chambers. She noticed the Recorder of London happily muttering to himself and she could have sworn that he said under his breath, '...and good riddance to bad rubbish!'

As Cecil was driven from court to start his sentence the jubilant heckling and banging of fists on the van were oblivious to him. He stared at the wall of the van in abject horror and shock. The guard who sat with Cecil saw the picture of a broken man before him.

He went to say something to console the prisoner, but then thought better of it.

Outside the court the cleaner was weeping whilst being interviewed by the press about her ordeal. Marjorie was further embellishing her lurid 'memories', emboldened as she was by the conviction of dear old Rupert.

Unseen in the crowds who vomited from the court building a lonely figure crept into what he hoped would be obscurity. But this was not to be the last for Giles Fitzmaurice KC. His fellow tenants left his chambers in short order followed swiftly by the clerks who were tired of being harassed by the media. He shut his beloved chambers down and kissed goodbye to his practice and any thoughts of being elevated to the bench. He met up for a drink with Bowers on the last day. They spent the afternoon in El Vino on Fleet Street reminiscing. Bowers felt desperately sorry for Fitzmaurice who was losing everything, and he thought saddest of all, he didn't deserve to – he just got unlucky. Soon afterwards Fitzmaurice's wife, mortified most by his apparent obsession with a 'cleaner' of all people, deserted him and used her own knowledge of the courts to thoroughly clean him out.

Some months afterwards he was interviewed by one of the more obscure tv channels about his fall from grace and his sudden rise to stardom or infamy. All being lost, he had decided to start YouTube and TikTok channels naming them 'Silky Sea Shanties'. They were supremely successful and went some way to redeeming him in the eyes of the public, particularly when he began drinking claret to excess during his shows. The more he drank the more popular his channels became. He was even named in some circles as a 'man of the people.'

A year later in a quiet ceremony in an ancient church in an even older village outside Windsor Fitzmaurice re-married ...to Marjorie, the cleaner! Bowers was his best man, and it was one of the proudest and happiest days of the clerk's life. The press had a real field day. They almost felt sorry for poor Fitzmaurice who had lost everything. The headlines about the marriage read variously, 'A real Cinderella story!', 'A match made in Hell!', 'Cocaine, murder, theft & love!', 'Wine swilling, shanty singing toff loses all, but still finds love!', 'His loyal clerk, his best man!' and 'She forgave all for love!'

The press loved him. They sold even more papers and

advertising than with Cecil's trial and Fitzy's fall from grace.

Fitzmaurice KC had not married her for love. He had married her for her large estate ...or at least the estate of Philip Cavendish which she had acquired. This had occurred following her production of a will which she 'said' she had found when going through some love letters the dead tenant apparently sent to her.

They honeymooned on the French Riviera staying at the Carlton Cannes Hotel and frequenting all the top restaurants and casinos whilst being followed by the ever-present paparazzi.

Oddly enough, Fitzmaurice did develop a healthy affection for her as the years passed, but it never surmounted his affection for her wealth or for the easy lifestyle it provided.

Happiest of all was Marjorie. She was filthy rich, married to a silk and they were both famous ...or as some considered, infamous. Best of all, she really did love Fitzmaurice!

Chapter Twenty-Four
HM Prison Wormwood Scrubs, London, U.K.

Rupert lay on the bunk in his cell. He was at the start of a very long sentence for a crime he did not commit. He was beside himself with shock and rage.

'Who did this to me!' he thought to himself.

He had widened the net from the initial suspicion that it was the police who had framed him. Now he suspected his wife, former girlfriends, former clients, colleagues at the bar, the odd judge here and there, of course his clerks, the media, some rogue madman, or woman who had taken against lawyers in general and still the police. Oh, and of course the, '...bloody cleaner!'

He was certain that some or all of them in some convoluted plot had conspired to destroy him ...but to what end?

Despite all his skills he could not understand why.

Epilogue
College Road, St Albans, Hertfordshire, U.K.

Cahill arrived home and hung his coat up on the rack in the hall before disappearing into the lounge where he collapsed into his Queen Anne style high-back wing chair. It dated from 1910 and was finished in a rich tan coloured leather with brass capped studs running around its borders. It was the only item of note that his family had managed to retain after his father's bankruptcy. It had passed to him following his mother's death and was his most treasured possession.

He was utterly exhausted. The barrister's murder enquiry had caused him much more strain than was usual.

Sitting on the table adjacent to him was a bottle of Château Lafite Rothschild 1998, Premier Cru Classe. He opened the opulent Claret, enjoying the slight popping sound the cork made as it was lovingly eased from the bottle. Then he placed the bottle back onto the table so that it could breathe for twenty minutes. As he waited, he spun the cork through his fingers, backwards and forwards taking in the smell of the wine's residue on one end of the ancient bark. The scent was glorious. He enjoyed drinking red wine but could never afford a wine of such quality. Savouring the aromas, he thought of the investigation and as he did so, he smiled. The case had made his name. But it had also done so much more.

Cahill's chair faced out into his garden and on the floor close to his feet was the copy of The Times newspaper he had brought home with him. The main article detailed, what the journalist called, the legal crime of the century, and the headline was written in large print across its front page. The article raved about Cahill's dogged skill and the diligence of the judge, jury, and the prosecutor. It spoke of the murder victim, mentioning his name and it also mentioned the callous killer's name.

'Or did it?' Cahill thought.

The paper slipped from his hand and dropped to the floor.

The D.I. looked towards the wooden side table which had pictures of his mother and father in happier times and another picture which lay face down.

He turned to the fine claret and picking up the bottle, sighing, he gently poured the exclusive red Bordeaux into a heavy crystal glass. The smell of the wine was intoxicating. He held the glass up to the light and savoured the deep ruby red colour which shone forth. As he drank from the glass, he felt that he had never before had a wine with such profound bouquet and body.

Looking out into the darkness of the garden he remembered back to a night, not dissimilar to that night, many months before when he had stealthily crossed a suburban garden much like his. Cahill remembered the cold wind on his skin at that time as he had disappeared into the wood, bag in one hand and the Claret in the other.

Returning to the present, he placed the glass on the table and then picked up his parent's picture as tears ran down his face. Cahill then said in a matter-of-fact manner, 'It is done my darlings!'

Next, he picked up the frame that lay nearby, flat on the tabletop. Opening the back of the frame he took the photograph out. It showed him at his upper school, or at least, the first one. It was taken in his first year. It was a class photo which had been taken before he was expelled. The image was a duplicate of the photo which had been crushed underfoot at the murder scene.

He stared at the photo which showed him as a happy young boy sat in a row beside his classmates and with his two best friends, one on either side. In the picture and to his left the face of the child beside him had been burnt out leaving a circular hole. He had defaced it with a burning cigar the night he had killed Philip Cavendish in his home.

Rupert Cecil had walked down the steps from the dock and into a prison sentence he would probably never survive. He had been destroyed as had his reputation. As Cahill sat in his chair celebrating, he could not help but reflect about the horrors that those two had visited on him and his family years before. He took a comforting puff of the cigar, then held it over the marble ashtray to his side before giving it a flick with his finger. A large tube of ash fell to the tray leaving the burning hot tip glowing in the darkened room. He then contentedly twisted the cigar in his fingers before pushing the tip through the picture of the boy who sat on the other side of him, saying 'It took me all these years to repay your treachery! Goodbye Rupert! Someone really should have told you both that lying was not ...decent!'

He thought back to the time as a child when he had been falsely accused of theft of one of his fellow border's monies. The headmaster accused him of taking a large sum of cash from the boy's locker when they were both still in their first year of upper school. He found out that his two closest friends had committed the theft and had left him to take the blame. He refused to give them up, though he expected that they would finally admit to their culpability. His parents were called to the school and the headmaster spoke of his disgust at the theft, but also of the young Cahill's lack of character in refusing to admit to his guilt. He was expelled, despite his fathers' protestations. Sometime later he had found that his friends had in fact implicated him for the crime to protect themselves.

He was the fourth generation of his family to board at the prestigious public school and his father took the shame of what had happened very badly. He was a merchant banker, and all of his public-school friends began to distance themselves from him as his work began to dry up. He eventually went bankrupt and drank himself to death. The boy had changed his surname to his mother's maiden name, Cahill, to separate himself from it all and because a plan had already begun to formulate in his troubled mind.

Cahills mother also lost her friends and found that her social circle shunned her. They moved into a rented flat in a council tenement, and he had to enrol in the local comprehensive school. He was bullied incessantly due to his former wealthy background. Then the hardest blow came when his mother died as he approached seventeen. She had never gotten over the trauma of it all and nor the loss of her beloved husband. Cahill joined the army as a paratrooper. The officer corps was not an option for him, given his past.

Next, he joined the police. But in all the years he never stopped following the paths of the two supposed friends who had caused his demise. They had washed their hands of him once he was expelled. As the years went by the intensity of his hatred only grew as did his desire for revenge. The more successful they became the more he loathed them.

Cahill remembered the burglar he had caught years before when he was a young rookie. He had offered to let him off if the villain showed him the tricks of his trade, foremost among them was how to pick locks and to crack safes. The man was an old lag and he had dreaded the thought of another stint in prison and so he proved very helpful to the fledgling officer.

Cahill learnt well and employed the techniques to break into Rupert's home while the barrister was away one day in Chambers. He took a pair of Adidas trainers from a cupboard and using a pair of scissors he damaged the sole of one of them. Just enough to make an impression identifiable. The DI carefully unscrewed the brass handles on Rupert's French doors, being careful not to smudge any of Cecil's fingerprints. Then he replaced the handles with another identical pair he had bought weeks before when he had first cased Ruperts property. The ball was in play and Cahill waited until the 10th of October before he set the rest of his plan in motion. It had to be on that specific day, for that was the same date that he was accused of the theft all those years before.

When the appointed day came Cahill killed Cavendish and then he removed the handles from the dead man's French windows and replaced them with the set he had taken from Rupert's home. They were both brass, but the match was not identical. However, the DI thought that it was good enough for a frightened housemaid to gloss over. He was right, nobody had noticed anything unusual.

Then he had searched Cavendish's home. The burglar had been very thorough in his education of Cahill. He had told him of all the cunning ploys people had to hide their safe's or their secret compartments. The DI had found Philips hoard of cash and some of his most lucrative stamps. He had taken enough for his own use and left some for appearances.

Cahill had found the two keys on the ring with the attached plastic fob with a Penny Black stamp design when he had first searched Cavendish's room in chambers. He had palmed them and had later slipped them into the desk drawer in Cecil's nearby room along with a few of the rare stamps from Cavendish's home. It was enough to convince Beddingham of Rupert's guilt.

Then all he had to do was to plant some of the stamps and cash in Ruperts drawer while he searched the barrister's home. He also slipped the trainers with their muddied soles into the room ready for Beddingham to find. Rupert had assisted him by trying to frame Bowers for the murder with the keys. He had also gotten greedy and took the envelope of stamps home. It was so simple and along with the other 'evidence' was enough to convict poor Cecil! He had Rupert's house searched on the

23rd of October. It gave him immense pleasure to see his former schoolfriend arrested on the same date that he had been expelled from school so long ago.

It had never been enough just to kill them. He had to destroy them. To expose them for what they truly were.

Suddenly he caught a faint whiff on the breeze as it wafted through the open French doors. It was the subtle floral scent of flowering currant bushes in his garden. The smell always brought him back to happier times when he was a child playing with his parents. They had had a row of those bushes in their garden and wherever he lived he always planted them.

He took a deep smell of the ancient claret as he leisurely savoured the intoxicating aromas. Cahill was wrenched from his pleasures by the sound of his phone ringing. Looking at the screen he saw that it was a number that he did not recognise. He was unsure whether to answer it or not, but on the fourth ring he did so. He said matter-of-factly, 'Cahill speaking!'

No one answered and the phone went dead.

The DI was thoughtful for a moment. Had he made a mistake with his plan, did someone know? He looked pensively at the phone. He could get the boys at the station to run the number through the database to find out what was known about the caller, but he felt that that might prove to be a mistake. Disturbed, he then pressed the buttons to return the call.

A nervous woman's voice answered, 'Hello ...hello, Detective.'

'Who am I speaking to?' he said in a rather too officious manner.

He knew the voice, but he just couldn't place it. Then the woman continued, 'I'm sorry ...I shouldn't have called ...but, well ...I just wanted to congratulate you ... about solving the case. We met at the hospital. You probably don't remember me? I was the Matron you spoke to.'

Cahill's frown disappeared instantly as he broke into a wide smile of relief, saying happily, 'Yes, I most definitely do remember you!'

She giggled before replying, 'I hope that you don't mind my calling?'

He replied softly, 'Mind! No, I certainly do not mind! You have made a great night even better!'

They spoke for over an hour and as their conversation ended, they arranged to meet for dinner the following day. Once the D.I. put down the phone, he felt an immense sense of contentment and a clear connection to the unexpected caller. He greatly looked forward, once again, to meeting Matron Edwards ...Phoebe!'

He rubbed his beard. He hated it, but it had been a necessity, along with the passing years and changed name, to hide who he really was. But smiling to himself he thought that the next morning, he would go to the

Turkish barbers in the market near where he lived. He had a close shave and subsequently presented a much more youthful look to a giggling Phoebe.

The disloyalty and the dishonesty and the years of pain had destroyed something good in him. But the divine hand of fate was watching. Preparing itself to redress the imbalance in the tormented man's life. It had something better in store for Michael Cahill and eventually the good in him would return, as would the joy!

AFTERWORD

Thank you for taking the time to read or listen my book. I hope that you enjoyed it.

You can greatly help me and potential new readers by leaving a review. As long or as short a review as you wish would be great.

I read all reviews and greatly appreciate the time and effort that my readers go to in leaving them.

If you wish to join my mailing list to be among the first to hear about forthcoming books and deals, then please sign up at: **www.idograf.com**

Thank you.

Ido Graf

About the Author

Ido Graf grew up in the Mediterranean and in the United Kingdom, predominantly in London.

After studying for a bachelor's degree, Ido went on to study for a masters, before taking other specialist qualifications.

He spent some time in military bases in Europe and the Middle East and comes from a police & military background.

Ido has travelled extensively in North & South America, Europe, Africa, the Far East, Russia, and the former Eastern bloc countries.

He was questioned at length in Guinea by the Presidential Guard on spying allegations relating to the Presidential Palace and in Sierra Leone by agents of the state concerning alleged diamond smuggling.

Ido and a friend of his once engaged in a shooting competition in the Củ Chi district of Ho Chi Minh City, with John F. Kennedy while Jr. Daryl Hannah watched the three of them as they fired AK-47s. It was an extraordinary, chance encounter when they were travelling in Vietnam in the 1990s.

Ido is a fully qualified scuba diver and skydiver. He is a proficient snowboarder, skier (both downhill and cross-country) and a highly experienced alpinist.

He has worked in various sectors for both government departments and private concerns in a variety of sensitive fields in the UK and North America.

Ido Graf is a writer of mystery and suspense thrillers. His works, which he is now publishing, are derived from his own experiences and from meticulous research. He visits all of the locations that he writes about to maintain the highest standards of realism within his novels.

Though much of his output is contemporary in nature, it frequently has a historical basis at its core.

The focus of his books is in the political, corporate espionage, thriller, and adventure categories.

He hopes that you enjoy his novels. Please follow Ido Graf on his blog:

https://www.idograf.com

Acknowledgements

Each of these people or groups have had an impact on my writing and on my will to write.

On some occasions, they may have felt that their contribution was minimal, but their impact was tremendous and at some moments, crucial.

Special thanks for their support, critical appraisal, guidance, and encouragement:

Family and friends including

My darling wife and my sons

Andy, Mark, David & Kerri, Ian, K.W., S.A.S.

Gerlinde

Inspirations

The many authors of fiction which I have read including, among others, such greats as Graham Greene, John le Carré, Frederick Forsyth, Nelson DeMille, Robert Harris, John Grisham, Jack Higgins, Mark Dawson, Thomas Hardy, Evelyn Waugh, Desmond Bagley, Hammond Innes, Helen MacInnes, Alistair MacLean, Robert Wilson, Randy Wayne White
and most of all the works and inspiring life journey of Lee Child.

The kindness, encouragement and tutoring of novelists: Frederick E. Smith and Rosemary Aitken.

Also

Special thanks go to those people, some I may never even have known or met, throughout my life who have extended to me - kindness, support, and assistance even though, on occasion, there was no reason to have expected it.

Any successes in my writing are built on the shoulders of those mentioned above, any faults are solely my own.